THE ANGEL OF
SANTA SOFIA

Josep Maria Argemí (Barcelona, 1965) is a writer and qualified lawyer who has published numerous exceptional novels and has been shortlisted for two of the most important prizes in Catalonia. He understands imagination not so much as a genre but as the prism that allows us to understand literature as a machine for producing happiness.

Tiago Miller (London, 1987) is a writer and translator based in Lleida. He has worked on a number of translations of Catalan writers such as Pere Calders, Mercè Ibarz, Jordi Amat, Raül Garrigasait, and the theatre company La Calòrica. His translation of Montserrat Roig's *The Song of Youth* was shortlisted for the Republic of Consciousness Prize for book of the year and the Oxford-Weidenfeld Prize for translation of the year.

This translation has been published in Great Britain
by Fum d'Estampa Press Limited 2023
001

© Josep Maria Argemí, 2021
This edition is published by arrangement with Lleonard Muntaner, Editor S.L.
All rights reserved.

English language translation © Tiago Miller, 2023

The moral rights of the author and translator have been asserted
Set in Minion Pro

Printed and bound by Great Britain by CMP UK Ltd.
A CIP catalogue record for this book is available from the British Library

ISBN: 978-1-913744-40-3

This work was translated with the help of a grant from the Institut Ramon Llull.

**institut
ramon llull**

Catalan Language and Culture

THE ANGEL OF SANTA SOFIA

JOSEP MARIA ARGEMÍ

Translated by

TIAGO MILLER

THE ANGEL OF
SANTA SOFIA

To the Orient of life I go.
To live in the Dream is to live in the world.
My path is lit by the glow
of loss, of souls ceasing to unfurl.
JOSEP PALAU I FABRE

We strolled between the walls and the fields
amid the black trees and shattered stones.
I had never seen a field so empty.
I felt the urge to be a swallow and fly far away.
CESARE PAVESE

1

I observed the rays of the setting sun glimmer above the snowy peaks of the Alps: akin to a miracle.

Closer still, the sound of the Po (the river reflected the nocturnal city like a mirror) was a familiar voice that revealed to me an incandescent mystery emerging directly from the swollen heart of the earth. As evening descended, I approached Turin. The twilight sky was aflame like a furious fire.

2

Beyond the hotel restaurant windows, a few black pine trees were silhouetted against the bleeding sky: the light ebbed theatrically with the deliquescent rhythm of a Wagnerian opera.

A waiter then served me a bowl of soup. '*Pesce cola*,' he said, winking at me. Shellfish. Submerged in the golden liquid was a red fish, its tail raised. As I ate the second dish (a cut of beef concealing its stringiness behind an ostentatious salad) a *signore* sporting an inquisitive gaze drew near.

'My name is Aymerich. I shall be participating in the Conference, just as your esteemed self,' he blared like a foghorn. I looked up from the steak and saw a man standing over me anxiously awaiting my response. For a few moments I considered feigning ignorance, of displaying overwhelming surprise, because *dear sir, I'm afraid you've mistaken me for someone else*. But I immediately realised that I'd only be encountering him over and over again in the lecture halls and corridors of the University, and that hoping to perpetually avoid him was foolish. Thus, I uttered: 'That is quite correct. I also study the Devil and his works.'

The man's gaze softened and we shook hands like two long-lost friends reuniting. And that was when I discovered, devoid of joy, that I'd have company at the Conference.

3

The following morning, before the baroque building of the University, an enraged mob vociferously opposed the Conference. The crowd brandished placards saying such things as 'ENOUGH LIES' or 'SOULS IN FLAMES'.

A couple walking past me on their way to the Conference commented: 'They're the parents of the possessed, demanding privacy and tact.'

The protesters' raspy calls scraped and clawed at the air. A few of them clasped their children by the hand, all of them pale, puffy-eyed, and whimpering with enrapture. Below the baroque frontispiece, the University dean smiled saintlike as he greeted the conferees.

4

Professor Piombo was himself a Doctor of Philosophy and Theology, a specialist in the works of the Desert Fathers, and a fervent scholar of the Dead Sea Scrolls. When he greeted me, his face (on account of the creases) had the appearance of an authentic palimpsest, as if traversed by the clouds of uncountable centuries but which had failed to erase his affectionate, almost infantile, smile.

He's a saint, I thought at first. But then after closer consideration: He's a man who hasn't lost his social graces. Groups of conferees constantly flocked towards him. It was almost as if they wanted to touch him (was that man, equipped with impeccable language and immaculate hands, an apparition?) so he might cure them of some dreadful disease.

5

The Demonology Conference was the brainchild of Cardinal Orsini, founder of the Athenaeum of the Archangel Michael, an organisation dedicated to the dissemination of Angelology (a 'Science linked to Music and Philosophy', as the cardinal would vaingloriously proclaim, while conjuring up the lofty ideal of Dante's Beatrice and listening – in his fanciful mind – to the lamentations of those condemned to the innermost chambers of *Inferno*), and staunch defender of the pre-eminence of the Church over the pathetic, crippled figure of the Devil. Nevertheless, the cardinal no doubt took pity on those poor souls possessed by the satanic spirit as they scratched the walls and tore at their rags along their spiritual voyage to the deepest of abysses.

Hence, it was the pot-bellied and chubby-cheeked Cardinal Orsini who presided over the Conference's inaugural session.

6

'*Carissimi fratelli*,' he began, throwing himself forthwith into his curial, exemplary opening speech: the cold reason of Dogma and the familiar warmth of Tradition (not the reason of Intelligence, the beautiful incongruity) constituted his ecclesiastical rhetoric. Cardinal Orsini – a living symbol of scholasticism dressed up in the Dutch gold of condescension – filled the University of Turin's *Aula Magna* with an unctuous, imperative verbosity that quoted Matthew, Peter, Luke and John as if those saintly men had personally revealed their secrets to him.

As the volley of words and sentences became increasingly cumbersome, subsequently losing their desired effect, his scholasticism slowly gave way to dramaturgy: a horror story, shrouded in an ashy mantle, in which Man first fights and struggles but is finally enslaved by the Devil, representing supreme arrogance and disdain; then came the good God, much like a benevolent echo resounding in the dark soul of night... The Cardinal played all parts cast in his impromptu play, moaning, pining, whispering, grappling with an invisible adversary, blinking like a startled moron, and reciting Saint Dionysus' prayer to protect himself from the Enemy.

A handful of nuns wept with devout joy in the front row of the *Aula*, a Greek Orthodox bishop sighed heavily as he contemplated the painted ceiling (where sweet angels and a pristine starlit sky hovered above the human condition) before rapidly thrusting his jet black beard towards the travertine marble floor, and Father Filipetti, the Vatican's eminent exorcist, sat saintlike with his eyes softly shut, immersed in the lethargy of profound meditation.

Floating in the form of background noise, the roar of the protesters and the cries of the possessed demanding justice could be heard. And that was when I suddenly recalled Apollyon's first teaching: *EX TENEBRAE LUX.*

7

Apollyon had first made his presence known to me in a bar.

The bar in question was somewhat of a refuge for the lost, wandering souls of the University of Barcelona and was located immediately opposite the neo-Gothic building where some venerable professor or other would be intoning canonical lessons to withered spirits first thing in the morning.

Vitality returned in that bar in mysterious ways: one student would be clutching the *Summa Theologica* while sucking gleefully on a glass bearing a liquid the colour of blood; another, still inebriated from the night before, howled something unintelligible; another jaundiced individual was submerged (noise simply didn't exist for that serious, solemn student) in the extraordinary reading of a thick tome of parchment papers decorated with sparkling silver letters; a few more frantically threw their cards down upon the table as though life (drawn on the playing cards flying from their hands) were burning their fingertips.

Another, propping up the bar, appeared to be sleeping. A waiter, as repugnant as a gargoyle, went over to him and said, 'Master, it's time.'

He opened what proved to be the strangest eyes I've ever seen: was he a man or a snake?

8

Apollyon imparted lessons on material not studied at the University: the language of birds, that primitive language spoken in Paradise; the topography of Hell, which was a planisphere of infinite staircases, innumerable corridors and bottomless pits;

the mysterious fate of beautiful Shahrazad, who wove stories to survive within a single eternal night; or the sacred nature of the phoenix, which died and emerged reborn from its own ashes.

9

'*Ubique daemon*... the Devil is all around us,' exclaimed Cardinal Orsini, ending his speech.

His proclamation of faith (in the existence of the Enemy) tore me from my daydreaming, as brief and as light as the fluttering of a butterfly's wings.

As the applause began to reverberate around the *Aula Magna*, I shot out in search of the nearest bar. Soon I was lost within the labyrinthine corridors of the University.

10

I wound up in the oldest part of the building, where the spirit of the House of Savoy had been perfectly preserved: the Kingdom's shadow lay thick over that secret museum full of suits of armour decked in royal insignias, portraits of Count Cavour on both foot and horseback, and engravings of the glorious victory at Marseilles where General Garibaldi knelt before King Victor Manuel.

I heard footsteps emerge from amid the fantasy and immediately sought refuge in an adjacent room, dark, silent and brimming with golden cornucopias.

The footsteps suddenly stopped. Two people, whispering the whole time, had entered the chamber without switching on any of the lamps. (I'd since wrapped myself in a velvet curtain behind a harpsichord from Mozart's time.) The two people were an elegant woman making graceful gestures accompanied by a man breathing like an asthmatic.

Sitting side by side on the sofa, their whispering lasted a long while before the man walked out, dragging his feet beneath him, leaving her in a sea of tears. So persistent was the woman's weeping that I simply couldn't resist playing the hero: I sprung forth from my hiding place and went over to the disconsolate *dama*. She didn't look at all surprised to see me. In fact, that chimerical room seemed the ideal place for ghostly apparitions. I offered her a tissue, which she accepted and used to dry her tears before saying, 'I'm Countess Sofia Pozzi. And I'm in need of assistance.'

'I'm Josep Palau i Fabre, researcher of the Extraordinary,' I answered. 'And I humbly place myself at your complete disposal.'

She smiled sweetly amid the shadows.

11

Countess Pozzi explained to me the reason for her desolation:

'*Signore* Palau, a great curse has befallen my family. A few months ago, Leonora, my daughter, suddenly fell ill. What seemed at first like a standard, albeit heavy, cold (however nagging) turned into something altogether different: bit by bit the bothersome fever transformed into a disturbing delirium, Leonora's physical feebleness reached such elevated levels of languidness that it surprised even her doctors, and every one of them venturing into her room (swathed always in darkness) to examine her stared with wild eyes before running back down the stairs mumbling excuses about urgent appointments, stuttering erudite ruminations full of Latin phrases, or distractedly mumbling prescriptions for natural potions and herbal remedies the ingredients for which were to be picked in the mountains under a full moon.

'One morning it occurred to me to call on a priest I'd known for many years, a friend of the family (he anointed my husband, who died from malaria after an expedition to China), who in turn entered my daughter's chamber with the confident, paternal gaze of a person possessing divine protection, only to run out of the room whimpering, "*Il Diavolo.*"

'I was sure the priest had lost his mind. The man, evidently distressed, asked for a brandy in an attempt to pull himself together. He drank and prayed, in that order, his prayers increasingly confused, tears pouring from his eyes, a forefinger feebly pointing towards the dark room.

'Before taking his leave a good while later (fully composed once again and looking vaguely embarrassed), he told me he would speak directly to the bishop. "An exorcism is required," he added with a voice that appeared to rise from the depths of the centuries.'

12

Countess Pozzi told her story with grief-stricken grace, a dark veil slowly descending over her voice.

'And, indeed, the priest spoke to the bishop but here I am, still awaiting his answer. "It's a very delicate matter," utters the honourable man with the air of someone concealing a secret each time he calls on me with an update and an excuse (and to gladly accept the sherry and cream cakes I offer him). Having been schooled in the strict art of patience, I must confess, *signore* Palau, that I've just about none left. That's why I came here, to demand – unaware if such a thing was even possible – an audience with Father Filipetti, the Vatican's exorcist. I presented myself before him like the desperate mother that I am and he gazed at me with saintly eyes as we lost ourselves along the corridors like a pair of dreamy *innamorati*. We came to this room bathed in darkness, so ideal for revealing secrets, and Father Filipetti listened to me for a long time with voluptuous disquiet before finally whispering a few words as though absolving me (which was when I realised he'd thought I was confessing my sins) and immediately left with the dilated pupils of a small bird.'

Countess Pozzi then asked if I'd be willing to visit her at the family *palazzo*.

'It's a question of life or death,' she implored.

13

That evening at the hotel, Aymerich bore down on me with his burning gaze.

'Is it *true* that you've already had dealings with Countess Pozzi?' he asked in an overly familiar, unctuous tone.

Before I'd had time to arrange my thoughts (could this impertinent conferee have followed me along the University corridors?), he continued.

'Why, everyone knows *signore* Sofia Pozzi is the leader of the Children of Satan, the parental movement that protects children *possessed* by the *Devil*. Some (well-meaning) people regard it as a mere self-help group, while others adjudge them to be promoting the destabilisation of the Church with the aim of forcing its fall into complete, universal disgrace, as if announcing some deformed manner of carnivalesque buffoonery through their poor, spirit-sick children.'

Annoyed by both the informality with which he had referred to the countess and the vulgarity of his tone, on this occasion I wasted no time in replying:

'There is a time to keep silence and a time to speak.'

Upon hearing the quote from the Ecclesiastes, Aymerich burst into snorts and guffaws as though I'd told him some sort of bawdy, barroom joke.

14

The following morning, there was a great *mêlée* in and around the University of Turin. The keynote speaker was none other than Doctor Magnus from the University of Uppsala.

Just as had been circulated in the months preceding the Conference, the talks would focus on the hypothesis of a 'World of Shadows' existing in symmetry with the Universe. Basing his thinking on subatomic physics, Doctor Magnus had constructed an entire theory on the antimatter that reflected, like the surface water of a lake, our palpable world.

According to Dr Magnus, that 'other world' – the reflection in the mirror – is where all the 'dark energy' in the Universe resided. Some even called it 'the Devil's energy'. The Swedish doctor entered the *Aula Magna*, climbed up onto the stage, and stared at the captivated audience with steel blue eyes.

Was he the prophet of a dawning age?

15

Doctor Magnus had silver hair, was dressed impeccably in white, and his hands seemed like those of a pianist devoted to the works of Chopin or Grieg.

With great precision, the subatomic physicist proceeded to present a monstrous machine: a sphere shining like a full moon in the centre of a web of cables that completely covered the speaker's table and carpeted the floor like a dystopic vision from a future world.

He then began to caress the sphere, first with tenderness, then with the insistence of an obsessed lover. Finally, the sphere responded with thunder and lightning.

After that, all was dark.

16

I walked along Carrer Mirallers, entered a doorway, and went anxiously up a stairway swathed in shadow. On the top floor, a gaunt, withered woman wrapped in a black shawl opened the door and led me into a stale-smelling bedroom. Two flames flickered along the fringes of the bed, as though I'd walked in on a wake. From the shadows, the mother watched over her child, who emitted a sickly moan. The parish priest monotonously recited the prayers *in articulo mortis*. The women cried and tugged ceremoniously at their hair. A group of anaemic children stared wide eyed at the child lying on the bed, who so resembled themselves.

17

The child in question was a girl who appeared to be sleeping. Her cheeks were as white as purest snow, her eyes sat softly shut amid the violet shadows, while her beautifully ruffled hair resting on the pillow made one think of imminent death. Suddenly, the girl opened her eyes and seemed to look at me before saying, 'You've finally come.'

I was about to answer the patient returning from the grips of death with some gallantry or other when I realised that standing behind me, precisely where the girl's gaze was directed, was a looming shadow.

It was a man with snake eyes.

18

Barcelona breathed a delirious dream. I walked streets that stretched out before me like ghostly spectres. From the barely half-open doors, all manner of whispers and invitations to pleasure and pain reached my ears. In the windows, anonymous hands making strange signals indicated meetings of secret brotherhoods.

Throughout the squares, the plague ridden who'd fled their homes huddled under the arches hoping to find there one last human caress before the inevitable end. Death rolled into the city, it climbed the putrid walls, it floated above the shattered stone and gorged on the yellowing grass. I followed the sick girl (now completely revived) and the mysterious man with bestial eyes. They strode forwards with a quick pace, soon leaving the scarred city walls behind to begin their ascent of Montjuïc. At the top of the path, the cemetery shone in the moonlight.

19

Between the monumental crosses and sculpted angels, and
below the cypresses overhanging the city of the dead, a crowd of
children sang and danced with unfettered joy upon the tombs.
The girl appeared hesitant, as if waiting for a sign from the mysterious man, before finally turning and saying to him, 'It's time
to play.'

The child skipped and capered like a cat on a drawing room
rug while the snake-man lay down on the tomb of an archbishop
whose sculpted marble hand was raised high in defiance of the
night to bless the children who'd been resurrected in that secret
paradise.

20

The cold morning light returned me to the *Aula Magna* at the
University of Turin. Doctor Magnus was finishing his presen-
tation. His machine – that sphere reflecting the dark energy of
the Universe – emitted the smell of sulphur. The audience, many
of whom had tears in their eyes, applauded fervently. I left and
staggered towards Bar Manzoni opposite the University.

The *prophet of a dawning era* now imparted his wisdom via
a drunk and somewhat disorderly discourse. The girls listened
in, each and every one of them enraptured by his mixture of
mysticism and ultra-modernism, trying to catch the great man's
words as if they were atomic sparks flying from his vast, insati-
able gullet. Dressed in traditional garb (starched white jackets,
black bow ties, wild moustaches à la Garibaldi), the waiters at
Bar Manzoni paraded past the wise man and offered him their

tributes: gin, scotch, vodka, and brightly coloured cocktails crowned with froth and sugar designed to pander to the spoilt children in adults.

The girls giggled at the spectacle.

One of them approached me. 'I trust you slept well during the talk?' she asked. But before I could utter a word in my defence, her compassionate gaze settled on Doctor Magnus. 'I am the wise man's daughter.'

21

Doctor Magnus' story was both sad and splendid (at least, that was how his daughter explained it to me).

Hans Magnus had been a wandering child who'd get lost on almost any available occasion: in summer in the sprawling oak grove near his grandparents' house, hanging on the flight of some bird, or the clouds as they sparkled between the leaves of the trees; in winter along the streets of Stockholm, as he walked out of the school gates only to become enchanted by the shiny shop windows (or the glow of the car beams) until he ended up in the most bizarre places; or in autumn when little Hans liked to run like mad through the rain before seeking cover in some antiques shop where he'd unearth an entire world of wonders such as a medieval *mapamundi* decorated with mermaids and dragoons, a music box playing human harmonies, an automaton from the royal collection said to have played chess against Voltaire... 'Childish nonsense,' his father would scold him later, a protestant pastor who preached on Sundays to devout Christians who admired the severity of the one true God.

22

Then pastor Magnus would punish his son by locking him in his bedroom with only a Bible for company. But Hans, far from afflicted by this measure, and always fascinated by any object (however small, and this one was enormous), immersed himself in its holy pages, delighting in Jonas' journey into the heart of the whale's stomach, in Elias' carriage as it flew towards the heavens like a fiery stallion, in the Pharaoh's Delphic dream that Joseph managed to interpret in clear, direct language, or in the dawn within the primitive garden at the centre of Paradise. When the punishment came to an end, Hans sat weeping tears of joy, and Pastor Magnus took it as proof that God really does work in mysterious ways.

23

When the fine weather arrived, Pastor Magnus would visit the villages skirting the Boren, Roxen and Glan lakes, for it was in this neck of the woods where he began his illustrious career as a preacher and where he still had a good number of friends and loyal followers.

The pastor's wife – who staunchly believed that the God of the Holy Scriptures was also present in all of Nature's wonders – insisted that her husband took Hans with him so that he might become acquainted with the lakeside villages.

Thus, that spring, Pastor Magnus went to preach the Word beyond the confines of Stockholm, and his son was enchanted by altogether different 'miracles': the carp as it leapt from the water, suspended in mid-air for an eternal moment; the swordfish as it sliced the water's surface like a streak of lightning; a turtle shell shining like an emerald lost along the banks… Hans the wild child collected all manner of hitherto unimaginable treasures there by the lakeside: the stem of a parasol mushroom that glimmered like snakeskin, a feather from the same white-tailed eagle that hunts sturgeon and otters, or a gemstone that sparkled like a black sun.

24

Back in Stockholm, Pastor Magnus received a visit from a blind parishioner.

That man – blind from birth, and who found solace in his readings of the Bible through the pastor, which he imbibed like holy music filling him with divine light – was content with his blindness. 'It was God's plan for me to be this way,' he would explain, claiming it was a sign from Heaven, while the pastor looked on and wept.

One fine day, while listening to a passage from Hebrews ('Neither is there any creature that is not manifest in his sight: but all things are naked and opened unto the eyes of Him with whom we have to do'), the blind man's face became like a 'living stone' because he had been wounded by a 'vision'.

The poor parishioner then contemplated the world for the first time: before him he saw Pastor Magnus' face ploughed by a thousand wrinkles and a fiery-winged angel stopping Abraham just as he was about to sacrifice his son Isaac in the painting that presided over the large home library where the Lutheran Bible, the mystical works of Emmanuel Swedenborg, and the fabulous tales by Brothers Grimm rested.

Upstairs, happily hidden away in the attic, the wild child played joyfully with the jet black gemstone he'd found along the banks of the lake. The mesmerising object shone like the promise of a new world.

25

Countess Sofia Pozzi's palace was located at the bottom of a street lined with old houses. The palace's façade was pockmarked, the blind windows had their curtains drawn, and the front door seemed more in keeping with a fairy tale than reality.

A servant with black gemstone eyes led me through a labyrinth of corridors laden with family memories: portraits of relatives hanging from the walls who stared back like owls watching from the treetops; flintlock pistols not used since the days when wolves and bandits encircled the Monte Leone manor; the ceremonial masks that the Countess' father had stolen from the burning deserts of Abyssinia…

Fantasy or reality?

The Countess received me in the manor's extensive drawing room.

'*Signore* Palau,' she whispered with as much velvety exquisiteness as the curtains that concealed the poverty and melancholy of that house, shrouded as it was in golden darkness.

26

As I entered the bedroom belonging to Leonora, the Countess' possessed daughter, the scene I was presented with didn't seem at all strange: the candles placed around the bed, the ghostly darkness engulfing the furniture and paintings, the mirror flashing in the corner…

Some while later (time thickened and slowed in that house so crammed with relics), I realised there were more people in the room, most notably three or four figures at the back of the bedroom reciting dark psalms.

'Those are the parishioners Father Filipetti sent me,' the Countess whispered into my ear before pushing me softly towards her daughter.

I contemplated the pallid, statuesque face of the girl lying on the bed. Beautiful in the classical sense, Leonora reminded me of a renaissance princess laid low by the ecstasy of love. As I drew closer to her pillow, her moans became mixed with words I was unable to interpret.

I leant even further forwards and heard the roar of a river, singing birds, a swirling wind… Nevertheless, one sentence could be heard above and beyond the primitive tumult: 'I'm coming.'

The girl's gaze rested on me. I rested my head on her pillow. Leonora showed me the dark depths of her soul.

27

Through Leonora, Lord Lucifer spoke to me: 'I'm coming to awaken the innocent souls still slumbering, to heal the afflicted, to make the world a more beautiful place. I am the Great Mystery, the Vast Unknown, the Indecipherable Enigma. I spread my hands and create a Paradise, my Language is a secret, my Will is dark. I hide in mirrors, at the bottom of fountains, in the centre of labyrinths. The motto on my coat of arms (I am a prince after all) reads 'I PLAY'. I have one hundred eyes to see the world and one fiery tongue to praise it. My blood is a deep river, my heart a beating volcano. I travel in search of the Eternal Moment. I herald the new world now beginning.'

28

I woke up feeling as though I'd slept for a hundred years.

Staggering through the parks of Turin, all I saw were shadows, despite the bright sun.

Far beyond the trees, on the horizon, I divined the flickering spire of a building rising majestically over the city and walked towards it through a labyrinth of streets. In a square that seemed to appear from nowhere stood the marvellous *Mola Antonelliana*, imperious and fantastic.

In that building, now housing the National Museum of Cinema, a singular event was being advertised: a series of old films intimately connected to the Demonology Conference. Like a pilgrim arriving at the temple of God, I walked inside with a heart bursting with expectation. I pushed the glass door, crossed the marble *atrio* and climbed its spiral staircase.

As I entered the dark hall, a screen seemingly made of silk displayed the stunning images of a forgotten art.

29

The films were silent shorts. The Devil's shadow floated above them all. *Circo Diavolo* (Piero Nero, 1921) was a delirious fantasy about a circus that shocked cities and villages with all manner of infernal beauty: the Man-Snake who dragged himself along the ground from the beginning of time when the Garden of Eden was the whole world; the Spectre who lived inside a glass bell and recited day and night King David's psalms, which the very monarch had taught him by the light of the fire; the beautiful Scylla who'd seduced Poseidon and continued to enrapture those who dared draw near her pool full of soft algae and sparkling stones; or Cybele sat upon her stone throne revealing fate thanks to the power of magic herbs. The ringmaster was Pan himself, always well accompanied by a long line of satyrs and nymphs that took horror and fascination with them wherever they went.

30

L'abisso (Gil Lanna, 1910) was the romantic, sombre story of a sentimental piano teacher thrust into the hands of a lion tamer (in the phantasmagorical *Circus Fortuna*), something another pretender – a love-sick fellow decked out in a frock coat, bowler hat and cane – was unable to accept. Thus, he joins the circus as a knife thrower.

Meanwhile, the tamer imposes upon her the same ferocious methods he uses on his savage animals. The piano teacher, lost in the dancing daydreams and sepulchre parks, is plunged into a delirium (in which she dreams of eternal love) after one of the two men (the lion tamer? the man in the frock coat? *ça n'importe pas*) is murdered in the crudest of manners in a squalid hotel room.

The murderer is never found.

31

In *Rapsodia Satanica* (Nino Oxilia, 1917) a widowed countess seeks a deal with the Devil (emerging theatrically from a mirror dressed as a cardinal of the Holy Roman Church): if the countess agrees to renounce love (represented by the figure of Cupid, who she is to smash to pieces), the Devil, magically moving a clepsydra, will return her her youth.

They close the deal and the countess is whisked (as if in a dream) off to a wild party. There, she sings and dances in a frenzy, and playfully seduces a couple of dandies with wandering, inquisitive eyes. The Devil, taking the form of a bird, observes the bucolic scene from the treetops.

Offended by some banality or other, a young gentleman at the party threatens her most unexpectedly: if she refuses to leave with him that very moment, he'll take his own life. She laughs and pays him no heed but when the man later commits suicide, the countess suddenly feels the full weight of time (up until that point the party had seemed eternal). She notes her wrinkles return, her spiritual languidness reaches neurasthenic levels, and she rediscovers the horror of mirrors.

The Devil, terrified by so much stupidity, flees both lake and woman to return to the taverns in the hope of doing more profitable business.

32

The lights came up.

In the last row was a man weeping. His ageless face (neither young nor old) was covered in shimmering tears that coursed from his scintillating eyes like the seraphim painted by the first Italians. Yet, beyond the artistic reminiscences, I was sure I'd seen that angel elsewhere; if I wasn't mistaken, at the Demonology Conference amid the many devotees avidly awaiting a sign from the Holy Spirit.

The man with angelic features greeted me as if we were old friends. In fact, we'd been the only spectators of those old satanic films, and I gladly accepted his greeting and posterior invitation to Bar Elena.

'I want to tell you the real story of the Devil,' he said, his eyes now dry.

33

The words spoken by Doctor Mefisto (such was the name of that individual who'd seemingly escaped from a Fra Angelico painting) had the echo of an ancient fable, a belief in which demanded the pure faith of children.

'When I first encountered the Student, (everyone at the University called him that, perhaps on account of his bohemian, absent appearance, or perhaps owing to the heavy tomes he always carried up and down with an almost erotic delight) I'd never seen such a beautiful person. Nevertheless his face had something noticeably supernatural about it: his gaze shone like the scales on the dragons of legends, his voice appeared to rise from the very depths of the seas like an abysmal echo of whirlpools and shipwrecks. I recall he was dressed as if that very moment he'd come from a fancy dress party. He donned an 18th Century frock coat *à la* Voltaire, a bow tie as worn by Pushkin at his fatal duel, and was wrapped in a black cloak befitting Gogol's tale. As I'd soon discover, he was a new character every day, all the while expressing himself in the tone demanded by his *maschera*: now a goliard making merry in a tavern, now a sibylline cardinal dragging the ecclesiastic purple through this hellish world, another day a pontiff dreaming of discovering Heaven in a hermit's cave.

'"They expelled me from Jesuit seminary school," the Student would at times confess in joyful tones. If I asked him the reason, he'd quote the poet Virgil (*Facilis Descensus Avernis*) and immediately run off to an underground bar to down drinks and devise the definitive History of the Universe.'

34

'"My blood is weak," the Student once confessed to me in his nocturnal drinking den, his bright bestial eyes reflected phantasmagorically in the mirrors above the bar. He drank and spoke as though in the midst of a dream.

'"I've seen the centuries flow past like an endless river, a stream of water with its spring far out of reach of memory. I witnessed the first days of Creation, when the colours contained a cruel purity and forms were mere archetypes lacking in definition, and the whole world was wrapped in a piercing, triumphant divine light that blinded me. That was when I retreated to the shadows. From there, History appeared to me like water pouring from a gulley into the chasm below, a rainstorm of stones, piles of shattered skulls, desert dust, the swords of princes, the blood of slaves and the agony of the innocent. I've seen History as a phenomenon eternally repeating itself; horror and beauty ever going hand in hand, as if they were siblings that looked at and recognised one another deep in the infernal abyss."'

35

'The drunken orator encouraged me to drink in accordance with his unbridled pace, but all I could manage was to sip from an everlasting whisky while listening to his eloquence with the attention that beautiful but sombre stories deserve.

'"Then blood called me and I leapt from the shadows into the flames and felt the beating of the world (our Hell on Earth), the flowers that wither immediately after revealing their secret, the gazes blinded by the rising sun (our one true monarch), the twilight flames that consume lovers... like a magic trick by the hand of Lord Lucifer."

'Then the Student outlined his criminal life to me.'

36

'In the style of a symbolist poet sated by absinthe, he said:

"Blood calls me constantly by the most diverse means, above all through the pious dead. On occasions, when committing crimes out of pure caprice (I maintain that murder is one of the *beaux-arts*) I feel the beat of life resound in my head, existence as an irresistible fantasy. I remember with horror the snow-white hands of a Jesuit priest (at the seminary school in Rome, replete with glimmering Baroque altarpieces and marble floors, where I'd fall asleep before Horatio's *Rhetoric* or Aristotle's *Metaphysics* only to be woken by the song of the starlings cutting through the early evening sky) who would pinch my arms and legs and pull my ears and nose in his murky study at the end of the corridor. From there the garden could be seen (while I bent over to receive my punishment), full of exotic plants that embalmed the night air with luxurious aromas. Wrath (not piety) imposed upon me a terrible necessity for vengeance. I became the most docile, unquestioning of students, one who silently senses his soft skin blush with cardinal purple, a happy slave of his master (whose trust he wants to win), further tormented by a poem penned in Latin verse *Ad Maiorem Dei Gloriam* before extending him a greeting (the priest was a devoted reader of Petronius' *Satyricon*) or perhaps, like a lover, thrusting forth a lush bouquet of woodland flowers (among which are hidden *belladonna* and wolfsbane), making the monster open his eyes wide, wider than ever before. But, alas, the dear Jesuit was an old man with a weak heart and his sudden death *in the odour of sanctity* raised not even the slightest suspicion…"'

37

'Then, in the style of the lovesick, the Student said:

"I remember Silvia's neck with passion, it making me think of a flower's delicate stem. I'd cross the park full of statues of the gods, climb the stone path lined on both sides by cypress trees, and announce myself, *ignis fatuus*, at her door. I gave her piano lessons. Silvia would always be waiting for me in the ample drawing room, as pale and as keen as ever. Her eyes shone feverishly as she began the first piece (one of Chopin's *Nocturnes*), which she'd draw out over the entire lesson. The windows of the large drawing room looked out over the garden, but the languid music she played on the piano with extraordinary fluidity (I'd never had such a talented student) overshadowed the room, turning it into a soft, velvety chamber where we shared both the pleasure of the music and our furtive kisses that galloped alongside the romantic, crepuscular music. Silvia suffered from tuberculosis, meaning Chopin was her hero and his music her path of liberation away from the graveness of life. That's why she obsessively pursued (as if possessed by madness) some form of transfiguration. One sun-kissed morning, the consumptive pianist's spiritual adventure reached its culmination: Silvia played Op. 69 No.1 (better known as the *Farewell Waltz*), spat a hefty pool of blood into her silk handkerchief, and asked me with the upmost economy of words to help her put an end to her pain. I put on my leather gloves and piously squeezed her slender neck, which emitted a borborygmus reminiscent of the melody sung by the legendary swan in its joyous moment of ultimate ecstasy."'

38

'Then, in the style of a demented child babbling its first words, the great Fantasist said:

"I recall Doctor Basileus' steely gaze in his clinic on the island of Kos. That's where they eventually sent me on account of my *delirium tremens* which I – like an actor of Greek tragedy who's heard the truth direct from the oracle's mouth – executed with blood-chilling serenity as only those who've been touched by the holy fire can. Doctor Basileus received me like a severe father: he himself (and, alas, none of the disciplined, dazzling nurses) applied the appropriate corrective measure for my disease: firstly, blinding me through hypnosis; secondly, injecting me with lithium carbonate to sedate me; and, thirdly, the tying of physical restraints so I might overcome my psychotic fever. But I'd free myself of them and run towards the ruins of the nymphaeum and the Temple of Apollo, hide myself among the herds of goats there, and climb the moonlit hillside towards the olive trees. When Doctor Basileus wanted to lock me in a cell forevermore, I fatally struck him with obsidian, as though we were the protagonists of some ancient ritual."'

39

'The Devil's fantasies had the sharp aftertaste of the finest Scotch whisky,' murmured Doctor Mefisto, as though still revelling in the Student's binge.

When I asked if he'd ever heard from him again, he merely answered, '*È disparito*,' while moving his hand in the air like a bird taking flight.

Bar Elena had since emptied, the streets were full of shadows, and Turin had turned into a city of spirits. We crossed the bridge over the river. Doctor Mefisto, who'd been limping the entire route, stopped to watch the dark flow of water before weeping in silence.

He then asked me to accompany him home, a request I accepted, convinced I was performing an act of charity.

40

The night had swallowed up the city, and as we arrived at the isolated old *palazzo* (a house at the end of the world) life appeared to have disappeared forever.

We crossed the threshold of that imposing castle reminiscent of the most haughty, reclusive fortresses. I thought I was dreaming when I stepped foot in the hall: as wide as a cathedral's nave, it was lit entirely by torches which, owing to the magic of several golden-framed mirrors (as bright as the gold on primitive Russian icons), exhibited a holy patina formed of chimerical shadows and created the effect of beings suspended in the air while giving a dash of colour to the velvet curtains beyond which lay rooms glimpsed only by virtue of the flickering flames.

We entered one such room: a library.

My astonishing host then set about recounting a true story from the early Renaissance.

41

'One midnight, seven hundred years ago, the funeral mass for the Christian soul of Agostino Di Sacromonte having finally drawn to a close, a knock came at the door of this very house, and the family living here (the disconsolate widow and her children, who only a short while before had gone to bed, exhausted by the pain and pomp of the interminable funeral rites demanded by the death of a foremost cavalier) woke up with a start as though the pandemonium came directly from Hell.

'The knocking didn't let up and when the butler asked who could possibly want to come in at that ungodly hour a vaguely familiar voice boomed: "It is I… I've returned from the Other World!" As the voice repeated those words (making the glass panes shake like a gust of wind), the widow, having not forgotten her late husband's promises of eternal love ("Love shall overcome death") as he lay in agony, ordered him to open the door at once. When the man walked inside, his eyes flickered like torches and he floated above the ground like a phantom.'

'The first thing Agostino Di Sacromonte did was embrace his wife in a colossal, terrifying manner (such painful pleasure left his widow in a magical state of enrapture!) just like the resurrected returning from the bowels of an abysmal underworld. Nevertheless, the ghostly man immediately shut himself in this very library and, three days later, ordered them to notify Bishop Apollonio so that he might reveal to him the truth about his journey to the Beyond.

'The bishop – a cousin of the Sacromontes – arrived in a fluster, dragging a church secretary behind him. They locked themselves in the library with the *resurrected soul* for the entire night. As a new day dawned and birdsong began to fill the garden, the door flung open and out came the bishop, as pale as a cadaver, the secretary, jaundiced and heavy-eyed, and Di Sacromonte, *more alive than ever*. The master's voice once again boomed like thunder: "We're leaving at once for Rome to demand an audience with the Holy Father!" Without further comment, the cavalier, bishop and secretary boarded a carriage, drew the curtains, and departed as swift as an exhalation.'

43

'While four thoroughbred horses drew Bishop Apollonio's carriage through the testing countryside, rumours of the revelation contained within it spread far and wide. It was a rumour whispered in monastery studies and palace gardens, a bellowing cry that spread through village and city marketplaces, a serene voice affirming that those hastening travellers possessed a great secret, nothing less than a treasure trove of words and visions that would turn the world upside down.

'When the mysterious travellers' carriage arrived in Rome, every nook and cranny of the Apostolic Palace was alive with the silent echo of the providential news. Some desperately wanted to see in it a diplomatic mission commissioned by the Emperor, while others suspected it was no more than a domestic affair, relating to the episcopate coffers managed by Apollonio. There were even some papal courtesans who believed the *vox populi* that proclaimed the travellers' transcendental task. The Holy Father more than lived up to the nickname he'd been given in Rome (*the man with the bronze mask*, on account of his impassive countenance amid terrestrial storms) and he calmly welcomed the new arrivals to the Eternal City before leading them into his personal library.'

44

'What was the secret message of those words brought back from beyond the grave by the ghostly man who, like the poet Dante Alighieri, had traversed each and every hellish circle? What hope was there for Humanity?

'When the library door opened and the men saw the bronze mask smiling, it was as though their stony hearts, lost gazes and icy hands had come back to life. The courtesans, servants, soldiers and grooms had gone to contemplate the Holy Father's face and witness Providence's plan first-hand.'

45

'The Pope exclaimed in an unwavering voice: "*Laudatio deo*, for our brother Agostino Di Sacromonte has returned from the dead like a new Lazarus."

'The crowd fervently applauded those joyous words. Then, causing widespread exaltation, the Pontiff proclaimed: "They have truly shown us the path to Paradise." At that very moment, a small group of cardinals (whispering "*Santissimo ac beattissimo domino nostro pape*, before your sanctity we are but slaves and servants…") grabbed the Holy Father and pulled him deep into the bowels of the Apostolic Palace. Later, Bishop Apollonio and his secretary were ordered to forever withhold the secret revealed in the papal library under punishment of excommunication.

'They searched high and low for Agostino Di Sacromonte, wishing to put him on trial for heresy, but the spectral man had *la fortuna del Diavolo* on his side, as Romans say. He who was but a shadow had vanished amid the innocent souls celebrating the good news of his Resurrection.'

46

'Agostino Di Sacromonte slipped through the nocturnal streets of Rome, vanishing amid the infinite night of beggars, drunks, and prostitutes. He approached the banks of the River Tiber and listened to nymphal melodies. He danced jigs and pavanes with the Capitoline she-wolf. He embraced Augustus, ferociously proclaiming the glory of Rome.'

47

'The following day, teeming with abundant life, he boarded a Venetian galley in the port of old Ostia that traded in the Orient. The captain had heard rumours of a wild *mad man* who'd caused a great scandal at the papal court (provoking a somewhat serious illness in the Holy Father after being subjected to the monstrous stories uttered by that *heresiarch*), but he was none the wiser, given his mental picture was of a shabby, glassy-eyed man, more in keeping with an Indian fakir or one of those saints that spend their days dreaming on the banks of the Nile, and certainly not a gentleman getting involved with a seafaring crew for the first time out of a desire for adventure: after all, the black cape, feathered cap and brand-new seven-league boots said it all.'

48

'The journey to Cathay, long like the life of an Oriental sage, represented a ceremonial path towards enlightenment. The days brimmed with symbolism: the shapes of the clouds, the constant sound of the waves, the wind's voice whispering a universal message... Superstitious to the core, the sailors noted the tell-tale signs of omnipresent Fate relentlessly hunting them down.

'Night was the kingdom of phantoms: one sailor (unable to forget the image of a child being swallowed whole by a crocodile in the Upper Nile) trembled always at the sight of sinister shadows on the ship; another (born on the island of Crete) often dreamt of a labyrinth inhabited by a harrowing beast with human eyes; a Sicilian member of the crew would shudder when evoking the sight of *Peix Nicolau* – the half fish, half man who destroyed ships – in the bay of Naples. Meanwhile, the other mariners laughed, gulped down Marsala wine, and longed for the women they'd known in all the ports of the world.'

49

'Near the Strait of Messina, an enormous storm caught them by surprise. Amid the pandemonium, an unearthly din that rose up either from the water's surface or plunged down from the sky – no one could be sure (it was like an enormous swarm of bees frantically changing direction in the air) – suddenly engulfed the poor crew, blinded by the increasingly swollen waves making the galley groan and lurch.

'The roaring gradually softened, as if the bees had given way to a flock of birds hovering above the ship, and the sailors heard shrieks come from beyond the impenetrable curtain of spray.'

50

'Winged creatures then appeared from within the billowing clouds: sensual women-birds with abundant breasts and flaming claws tore at the air as though wanting to rip open the gates to Heaven while howling above the galley crew's heads.

'"The Siren daughters of the river God Achelous!" screamed the Sicilian sailor, clinging white-knuckled to his oar, his mystic gaze aflame.

'Despite the raging storm, the Sirens' song grew ever louder, penetrating the men's hearts, and they had to fight the mad desire to leap overboard and embrace the beasts.

'That was when a thunderous voice imposed itself upon the infernal din of the waves and the Sirens' ineffable throb: the adventurer in the black cape, who'd remained silent during the entire voyage, shouted a handful of words in an unknown language, and the sea fell immediately silent.

'The Sirens fled back towards the abyss (from whence they'd come), amazed at the sight of a man speaking the language of the birds.'

51

'From that moment onwards, the crew began to fear the adventurer in the black cape, who they'd come to name the *Immortal* on account of how he'd faced down the sea monsters and won. 'The *Immortal* spent his nights awake, attentive to the waves, as if expecting the imminent return of the Sirens, whose voice he seemed to know so well.

'On rare occasions, the mysterious man would speak with the captain, the two of them tracing the ship's passage together: his knowledge of astronomy was astounding, as though nothing in Heaven or on Earth were hidden from him.

'During the day, the *Immortal* was naught but a shadow that slipped past the other sailors, who never caught sight of him when he was near yet always *sensed* his presence, as though he were a figurehead forever fixed on the horizon.'

52

'Leaving Cyprus behind, they headed into an unmoving sea, a kind of dead lake lying lifelessly under a white, burning sky. The sailors felt their oars sink into a sandbank, while the heat seared them as if they were in the midst of a desert crossing.

'It's not surprising that during that strange sea voyage the men witnessed a wide range of mirages: a city in flames burning on the horizon, an army on horseback advancing through the clouds, Leviathan's formidable face rising up before them... In keeping with these illusions, the mariners espied a man clinging to a capsized clinker being dragged by the current like a floating albatross.

'They pulled him on board. That very evening a great deluge besieged them.'

53

'The man was emaciated, moaning unintelligible words. Everyone had the impression they'd seen him someplace before: some recognised a *pater familias* with pale cheeks who had died solemnly after blessing his descendants; others saw in him (however much against their will) a cruel, old man cursing his avaricious relatives covetous of his money and property; some observed a lost childhood friend, pure and innocent, his eyes like two wandering stars; others still were overawed by his face (so similar to a brother lost to the plague), the image of a ghost emerging from the sea like an eternal enigma.

'The sky turned dark and the silence thickened around the shipwrecked man pulled from the sea. Meanwhile, an immense storm drew ever nearer.'

54

'Then the captain spoke: "*La morte è presta.* Death is near." And he immediately led the man down into the hull to save his crew from hearing his gruesome moans.

'His laments, however, didn't cease, and instead fused with the creaking planks, clamouring sails, and howling wind. But the seamen still heard his moaning (the resulting fusion creating a sort of secret language) and feared his voice as if it were an immediate threat to their lives, even more than the rapidly approaching storm.'

55

'Encircled by resplendent bolts of lightning and rolling thunder, Agostino Di Sacromonte – who'd escaped the cataclysmic claws of Death and vanquished the Sirens – slipped off under a starlit sky to the hull of that Venetian galley to learn the dying man's *real and true* story:

"I remember the glistening light of Greece drenching the fields in drops of golden honey. I remember the darkness of the cave where I was born amid the huddling goats. I remember the ruins of the Temple of Apollo, crawling with lizards and overflowing with weeds. I remember the sweet song of the nymphs beside the fountains, a music that filled the entire world. I remember the fire that devoured the olive trees and obscured the sky. I remember the silent city streets where cicadas were no longer heard in the daytime, nor the owls at night. I remember my brothers, beggars all of them, unsurprised by the monster I'd become. I remember the lonely paths where time was as long as eternity itself. I remember a tiny village in India where I made snakes dance before the fire. I remember the Black Forest where I conversed brotherly with wizards and witches. I remember the *scriptorium* in a monastery high up in the Alps where a monk invoked me in front of a mirror that shone like the sun. I remember a Roman princess with golden hair whispering my name in a dream and I went to her and loved her *until the end of time*. I remember an irate crowd dragging me along the ground, an exalted multitude shouting 'Kill the Devil', a heartless mob launching me into the furious waters of the Styx..."'

56

'The man's delirium lasted through the night. Agostino Di Sacromonte had recognised him immediately: when he travelled to the Beyond (a grand palace with bedrooms and drawing rooms multiplying towards infinity, just like the reflections cast by a cornucopia), he'd heard his wandering footsteps along the corridors, the eternal rambler's exhausted breath, the ancient god's lustrous face. His name was Dionysius, though he was known, too, as Baal, Luzbel or Lucifer. Once high priest to Venus, the Morning Star, he was now a phantom tirelessly traversing the tenebrous paths of Universal History.

'It was there, in the hull of a Venetian galley travelling to the Far East, that Dionysius vanished – just like the character from the ancient fable who dissolves into the thin night air.

'Meanwhile, the ship was approaching Constantinople.'

57

'The captain received the warning not to dock in the Golden Horn due to a plague epidemic having taken hold in the city. Sprouting in the Hippodrome like a malignant flower, it had proceeded to spread, day and night, through the baths and churches.

'Seen from the galley, *Nova Roma* rose above the horizon like a silent, ecstatic vision. The great hum of the city – the eclectic voice of an entire civilization – had been snuffed out under the pale morning sky.

'Out on deck, Agostino Di Sacromonte had his eyes fixed on the Church of Santa Sofia as it reflected the first light of dawn. At that precise moment, the man who'd defeated Death thought he could hear the bronze angel of the dome whisper into his ear: "Dear friend, tell me of your journey to the Beyond."'

58

'Agostino Di Sacromonte wanted to impress the angel of Santa Sofia with words that burnt like fire:

"I dreamt I'd died. I wandered through a city in ruins before appearing in front of a half collapsed palace with a front door displaying fantastic animals that I recalled having seen long before when flicking through books in my grandfather's library (perhaps a bestiary containing prints with bright colours, perhaps the memoirs of some adventurer who'd arrived at the end of the world where monsters live). Sitting proudly on the door were a griffin, a basilisk and a whale, whose voices I seemed to hear intoning hitherto unheard melodies inviting me to enter that mysterious mansion. In I went, but instead of finding a tomblike darkness popping with the sound of work-hard worms, I was greeted by the music of a *zarabanda* echoing throughout the palace."'

'"A great party was underway in the dreamhouse. Under the music's rhapsodic spell, I climbed a flight of stairs that led me into a chamber lit solely by torches, the inhabitants of which danced with the eternal harmony of celestial spheres. The dancers were like many-coloured stars evolving with great naturalness and elegance. Their faces flickered like flames (meanwhile the torches concealed the eternal night that had led them there), their hands fervidly caressed the air, and their feet were but seconds from taking off like scattering birds.

"The guests whispered all manner of secrets in some Adamic language from the age of miracles when lions conversed with sheep, and paradisiac birds chirped their ineffable song."'

'"Far beyond the hum of the party sat a man alone in a library. Angelic in appearance (hands as white as ivory, eyes the colour of pomegranate, an unseamed tunic befitting cherubim and seraphim), he was writing on piles of ancient parchment with letters of fire.

"The library was as large as the world itself. From amid the sum of all things (family geneses, mythological sagas, thousand-year-old hecatombs…) came the sound of whispering jungles, the deep murmur of rivers, and the roar of oceans, yet in the middle of that cacophony (it impossible to determine if it emerged from the illuminated bibles, chivalresque armorials or possessed encyclopaedias) the angelic man's thunderous voice dominated all: '*L'Inferno non è più.*'

"The man's writing lit the entire library.'"

61

The following morning, I walked out of the old *palazzo* but inside me I could still hear the same echoing words: HELL DOES NOT EXIST.

Up in the sky, Venus shone brightly, while the city slept within a deep dream of immortal love. In Piazza Carlo Felice, I saw Apollyon walking with quick, light steps. I followed him like a shadow dying in the dawning day.